P9-DHI-394

THE CRAFTERS' CLUB

TWO WORLDS
BOOK ONE OF THE CRAFTERS' CLUB SERIES

AN UNOFFICIAL MINECRAFT NOVEL

LOUISE GUY

This book is not authorized or sponsored by Mojang AB, or any other person or entity owning or controlling rights in the Minecraft name, trademark or copyrights.

Copyright © Louise Guy 2015.
First edition: 2015.
Printed by Go Direct Publishing Pty Ltd.

All rights reserved. No part of this book may be reproduced, stored in a retrieval system, or transmitted, in any form or by any means, electronic, mechanical, photocopying, recording or otherwise, without the prior permission of the copyright holder, except in the case of brief excerpts in critical reviews or articles.
All enquiries should be forwarded to
enquiries@godirectpublishing.com.
All of the characters in this book are fictitious, and any resemblance to actual persons, living or dead, is purely coincidental.

Print ISBN: 978-0-9943414-0-2

Edited by Kathy Betts
Cover design by Lana Pecherczyk

For the real-life JJ and Jamie.

*Providers of inspiration and insight
into a wonderful fun-filled world.*

CHAPTER ONE

Doorway to a New World

"I don't know why we let you be part of our Crafters' Club, Annie. All you ever do is wander around collecting food and eating."

Annie shifted in her beanbag and laughed. Her eyes were still fixed on the huge television screen. "What's wrong with eating? I wish I had a real cake, I'm so hungry."

JJ shook his head. "Help us finish the house. We still need to fix the roof and add beds before my dad comes and kicks us out."

Ten-year-old JJ, his seven-year-old brother Jamie, and their two neighbors, Charli and Annie, had started the Crafters' Club the previous Christmas. The club was based on their favorite game, Minecraft. The boys had received an Xbox from their grandmother and they all loved playing the game. They met most days after school and often on weekends to explore new maps, compete with quick builds, and to play Hunger Games. Sometimes they'd crowd around JJ's computer and watch him play on a server, but most of the time they preferred to use the Xbox where they could split the screen into four and all play. The girls, nine-year-old Charli who lived next door, and ten-year-old Annie who lived across the road, loved escaping their own families to be part of the Crafters' Club.

As usual, the walk home from school had been filled with Minecraft discussion. They would build a luxury house. Everyone was allocated a section and, as they did most afternoons, they hurried down their street to get started.

An hour later, the house looked amazing. It boasted a huge entry, movie theater, disco, indoor pool, library, and a massive bedroom with four beds. Jamie continued working on a lookout tower while Charli added a deck. JJ was finishing the glass roof and once the beds were made it would be complete.

"Oh fantastic," JJ said. He could hear his dad's footsteps approaching.

"JJ, time to turn the Xbox off and go outside. I'll bring you a snack soon." JJ's dad stood in the doorway of the room, his arms crossed. "Did you hear me?"

Of course I heard you, JJ thought. I hoped if I ignored you, you'd disappear. "A few more minutes and we'll be done."

"Two minutes, okay? Or I'm turning it off."

JJ waited until his dad left. "Sorry guys. Let's be quick. I'll put the beds in."

JJ expanded his window to full screen. Once he finished placing the beds he took the others on a quick tour through their latest creation.

"Awesome," Jamie said. "How good

is the lookout tower? You can see for miles."

"The library's amazing too," Charli said. "I put in heaps of shelves and books."

They could hear footsteps. Their two minutes had passed.

JJ saved their build and switched off the Xbox. "Come on, let's go down to the forest." It would give them time to work out what else they could add. A moat around the house would be great. "I found a way you can use a moat to kill mobs. They get trapped underwater and drown. With luck we'll be allowed back on the Xbox later."

Jamie, Charli, and Annie followed JJ out the back door and into the forest at the bottom of the yard. They slowed down when the forest became thick and difficult to walk through.

Annie hesitated as the others walked in further. "Are you sure we'll be safe in there? It's a bit overgrown."

Charli laughed. "A bit? Haven't you ever been down here?"

Annie shook her head.

"What, never?" Charli asked. "Why not? You've lived here for ages now."

"My dad told me to stay out. Something happened to Noah and Joe Wilson in there. Dad saw them come running out bleeding and covered in dirt. He's pretty sure they blew something up but he never found out because they moved a week later."

"I heard the same," Charli said. "Except I heard they moved because their dad got a job someplace else."

Jamie picked up a stick and threw it. "Who cares why they left. The main thing is that we find what they blew up. How awesome. Let's go and find it."

"No, I'll get into trouble, big trouble," Annie said.

"How's your dad going to know?" Charli asked. "We won't tell him if you don't."

"I don't think I should risk it." Annie remained behind the group.

"You don't have to come with us," JJ called. "Wait here if you want to." He turned to Jamie. "Head to the clearing on the other side of the creek. The Wilsons' built a tree house near there. It might give us a clue."

❧

Annie changed her mind and ran after the others. Fallen branches slowed their progress as they picked their way through the dense forest. They pushed overhanging vines and cobwebs out of their way. Once they reached the creek they followed Jamie's lead, stepping from rock to rock, avoiding getting their shoes wet. They leaped from the last rock and climbed the steep bank. A light shone through the trees.

JJ moved a branch and made his way around a wide trunk, expecting any moment to step into the clearing. Instead he crashed into Jamie's back. "Ouch." JJ rubbed his chin. "What are you doing? Why did you stop?"

Jamie stared ahead, silent.

"Why have we stopped?" Charli asked as she and Annie caught up to the boys.

Their eyes followed Jamie's finger to where he pointed. On the far side of the clearing, a fuzzy purple light flickered within a giant door frame.

"What's that?" Annie asked.

No one answered. They continued to stare at the unusual sight.

"I said, what's that?"

"It looks like a Nether portal," JJ replied. "But it can't be."

Jamie started to walk closer.

"What are you doing?" JJ grabbed his brother's arm, stopping him.

Jamie shook his arm, trying to free JJ's grip. "Let go, I want to check it out."

"No, you might get hurt."

"Do you think the Wilson brothers made this?" Annie asked.

JJ shrugged. "Maybe, or perhaps they found it. Why wouldn't they tell someone though?" Something happened to leave them dirty and bleeding. Whatever this was, it couldn't be a portal, someone had obviously gone to a lot of trouble to create something so similar. He scanned the clearing looking for a power source. "Okay let's get a bit closer." He let go of Jamie's arm. "Walk around, find out if there's a battery pack or something."

JJ took a wide path around the purple light to the other side.

"Listen." Charli stopped as an eerie noise surrounded them.

"Minecraft portals make the same weird noise," Jamie said.

The four walked around the doorway until they reached the other side. The back was identical to the front. There was no power source.

"Let's throw something in," Charli said, "and see what happens."

JJ picked up a rock and threw it at the purple light. Sparks flew as the rock entered and a small hole appeared before closing back over.

"It's gone," Annie said.

"Gone?" JJ walked back around.

He expected to find the rock on the ground. The grass was clear. The rock had disappeared.

∽

They each picked up sticks and rocks and threw them into the portal. Like the first rock, they disappeared.

"Awesome," Jamie said. "I'm going to try."

"What do you mean?" Charli asked. "Throw another rock in?"

"No, I'm going in. I want to see what's on the other side."

"No way," JJ said. "You might electrocute yourself."

"How do you know?" Jamie kicked the dirt at his feet.

"I don't. Whatever this is, it's not safe. Let's get out of here."

"He's right," Charli said. "What if it leads to the Nether? You might end up in a lava lake."

Jamie's face turned red and he clenched his fists. "What's wrong with you guys? This is the most amazing thing ever. You're all too chicken. Well, I'm not. I'm going in. I'll come straight back out to prove it's safe, then we can all go in."

"No," JJ said. "It's a crazy idea."

"Lucky I'm crazy," Jamie said. There was no time to stop him. He turned and leaped into the purple light of the portal.

CHAPTER TWO

Exploring the New World

"He's gone," Charli said.

JJ's heart raced. A few minutes went by. Nothing happened. Jamie didn't reappear.

"What do we do?" Annie asked. "Where is he?"

"Wait another couple of minutes," JJ said, "he's probably exploring. You know what he's like."

"What if he can't get back?" Charli asked. "We need to go in and get him."

JJ didn't respond. There was no guarantee any of them would get back if they followed Jamie. He checked his watch. Five minutes had already passed. "Okay, I'm going to go in and try to find him. You girls wait here."

Annie's lips trembled. Her pale features mirrored his feelings. He swallowed hard to push down the lump forming in his throat.

"Hold on, why are you in charge?" Charli's face flushed red. "If you're going in then so am I. You're not the boss."

"I never said that I was, but Jamie's my brother. If something happens I need you to be able to get help."

"Annie can go for help."

Annie frowned. "I'm not staying in

the forest by myself. One of you has to stay with me."

JJ and Charli exchanged a look.

"How about we do this," JJ said. "I go in and find Jamie. If there's no danger, and we can get back out, then we'll all go in together."

Charli nodded. "Okay. How long do we wait until we call for help?"

"Ten minutes. Then go tell my parents. Tell them to contact the Wilsons. Joe or Noah might know something."

"Why don't we contact them first?" Annie asked.

Jamie had been gone for too long. His parents would kill him if anything happened to his little brother. "No, I'm going in now. Wait for me here." JJ turned from the girls and approached the purple light. He knew he was crazy going after Jamie, but this whole thing seemed crazy. Perhaps he'd wake up soon and find it was all a stupid dream. He took a deep breath and stepped into the light. Something grabbed his arm as the force sucked him in and propelled him forward. Intense colors blurred around him as the grip on his arm tightened. The sensation stopped.

JJ stood on a hill, high above a treelined valley. The trees were different, yet familiar. So were the hills and landscape. It was nothing like the forest he'd come from. The world around him was built from blocks.

❦

"Wow, this is amazing."

JJ turned. Charli and Annie had followed him. They no longer looked like normal people but he still recognized them. He was looking at their Minecraft characters, Charli9, and CakeGirl1. He looked down at his body, JJLee45's Minecraft skin was now his own.

They stared at each other.

"What are you doing? You said you would wait," JJ said.

"And, like I told you, you're not the boss," Charli said. "We wanted to come, didn't we, Annie?"

Annie shook her square head back and forth. "No, you grabbed my hand and dragged me in. I didn't want to come."

Charli laughed. "Now you're here

you can thank me. Check this out, it's like we've entered a map in Minecraft. I wish I'd spent more time on my skin," she complained. "I look boring. Look at Annie's long aqua hair and her cake-girl body. She looks so cool."

"Let's not worry about our appearance," JJ said. "For now we need to find Jamie and work out how to get home."

"How do you think we do stuff?" Annie asked.

JJ wondered the same thing. He lifted his arm as he stepped forward. "I can move my arms and legs just by using them like I normally would."

"Hey," a voice called to them, "I'm down here."

They peered over the steep cliff edge to the valley below. JamieG14 looked up at them.

The tension drained from JJ's body. Jamie was okay.

"How do we get to Jamie?" Annie asked. "It's a long way down."

"If we were playing on the Xbox we'd just walk down," Charli said. "Come on, I'm going to try." She made it look easy as she weaved from block to block. She reached the bottom and looked back up at them. "Start walking," she called, "your legs go faster on their own."

Annie hesitated.

"Are you okay?" JJ asked.

Annie's mouth turned up into a small smile. "I think so. You go first, I'll follow."

JJ walked slowly at first. Then, as Charli had said, he found his legs wanted to go faster. It was as if he were jumping on a trampoline but without any effort. Moments later he stood at the base of the hill next to Charli and Jamie. Annie soon caught up.

"This is awesome," Jamie said. "Can you believe we're here?"

"Why didn't you come straight back out?" JJ asked.

"I wanted to look around. The portal disappeared when I came through anyway, didn't you notice? I arrived on the hill but when I turned back the portal was gone. I figured if I couldn't come back I might as well explore."

"What?" Annie's high pitched squeal

made JJ jump. "There's no portal to get back through? Are we stuck here forever?"

"No." JJ spoke in a firm voice. He didn't know how they would get out but the last thing they needed was for Annie to panic. "There'll be a way out. Your dad saw the Wilsons return so we know it's possible."

Annie's eyes filled with tears.

"Don't worry, we'll work it out." JJ sounded more confident than he felt. He knew nothing more than she did.

❧

Jamie punched at the air.

"What are you doing?" JJ asked.

"Seeing if I can break something." Jamie continued to punch out in front.

"All you're punching at the moment is air. You're not breaking anything."

"Should I try a tree? We might need to craft some things to help us."

"Like what?" Annie asked.

"I'm not sure," Jamie said.

"Punch the tall grass first in case you hurt your hand," JJ said. Learning to exist would be essential if they couldn't get back immediately.

Jamie moved to the long tufts of grass. His fist clenched, he punched out at them. Nothing happened. He looked up at JJ. "What am I doing wrong?"

JJ shrugged. "Try again."

He tried again, still nothing.

JJ walked over to Jamie and punched the grass. Nothing. He stood a moment then smiled. This time, he angled his hand down and punched. The grass broke and small green seeds floated above the ground.

"How did you get the seeds?"

"Don't punch in front, aim at the ground. Hit it like you do in the game. A block needs to be highlighted first."

Jamie tried again. The grass broke off and the seeds floated. He walked into them. They disappeared as soon as they touched his skin.

"Where did they go?" Jamie approached a tree. He punched again and again until blocks of wood floated near him. Each one vanished as it connected with his skin. "They must be going somewhere," he said. "We need to find out where so we can use them."

"They should be part of our inventory." JJ collected his seeds too. "But I can't find it. Can any of you?"

They looked around for their inventory. Nothing.

Annie turned to JJ. "Shouldn't we be concentrating on getting out of here?" Her voice shook.

"Yes, of course," JJ said. "Getting home is our number one priority."

❦

Jamie continued to punch down trees while JJ considered their next step. They needed to find a portal and get back home. If they couldn't find one when they played on the Xbox, they'd make it.

It would be simple enough if they could find their inventory. Obsidian blocks and flint and steel, and they'd be done. He sighed. They'd entered what had looked like a nether portal, so why were they in this place? This wasn't the Nether.

He looked across to Annie and Charli. Annie stared straight ahead and looked like she might start crying at any moment. Charli explored, walking down different pathways on the hill, stopping occasionally to look out across the landscape.

"Look." She pointed to the horizon. "I can see a house. It's the one we built on the Xbox."

In the far distance, a house sat next to a lake.

"Jamie, come and check this out," Charli said. "The lookout tower you built is massive, and I can see the glass roof JJ put on the house."

Jamie raced over to Charli. JJ and Annie hurried toward them.

"She's right," Annie said. "It looks exactly like the house we built."

"We?" Jamie said. "Eating cake isn't my idea of helping."

"Okay, cut it out," JJ said. "We need to work together as a team and figure out how to get out of here." He pointed to the house. "I think we're in our own map."

"Cool," Jamie said. "This is so awesome."

"No." Annie stamped her foot.

"This is scary and creepy and I want to go home."

"Be quiet, would you?" Jamie said. "Your whining is getting annoying."

"Jamie, I said cut it out." JJ turned to Annie. "Don't worry," he reassured her, "we'll get home." He smiled, hoping his confidence would help her relax. He was surprised the others weren't freaking out too. His own insides were turning to jelly. "So, first step, how do we access our items to build a portal? If we can find our inventory we can start building."

In the normal world the Y button on the Xbox controller would display it. They had no Y button here.

"Let me look at you." JJ walked toward Charli. "Maybe there's a button or something to give us access." Charli stood still as JJ looked over her character's skin. "Nothing."

"Hold on," Jamie said. "How does this work?" He lifted his arm to reveal a small electronic pad on his wrist.

"How did you get that?" JJ asked.

"I did this." Jamie punched his forearm and the device disappeared. He punched his arm again. The device reappeared.

JJ punched the same area on his arm, as did Charli and Annie. Their Minecraft skins opened up and their devices appeared. A blank screen stared at JJ. He touched the button on the top and the screen lit up. In his inventory, seeds filled one of the boxes.

Annie let out a deep breath and smiled. "Thank goodness, we can build the portal now and go home."

JJ eyed Jamie and Charli. Getting home wasn't going to be easy. He wondered how long it would take them all to work out what he just had.

❧

"Cool," Jamie said. "I've got heaps of wood blocks and seeds. Look," he tapped the device, "I can see my health bar and my hunger bar too."

Annie was the first to notice. "My inventory's empty," she said.

"Mine too," Charli said. "Except I can see my health and hunger bars. We're not in creative mode, are we?"

JJ shook his head. He could see his bars too and suddenly wished he couldn't. "No, I think we're in survival."

"Is that good or bad?" Annie asked. "Tell me it's good, because you're beginning to freak me out."

"Beginning?" Jamie laughed. "You've been freaked out since we entered the forest."

"How come you're not scared?" she asked. "Don't you care if we're stuck in here forever?"

Jamie shrugged. "Nope, means no homework and no yucky vegetable lasagna for dinner."

"Well, I don't want to stay here, I want to go home. JJ, please tell me you can make a portal?"

JJ looked around. They were in no immediate danger. "I know how to make a portal in survival mode but there are a few tricky bits. We need a diamond pickaxe for starters, which won't be easy. Survival is a lot more work."

Annie paled.

"Don't worry," JJ said. "The main thing is that we know how to make one. We need to explore, find the right stuff. It's no problem." No problem, who was he kidding? Not himself, that was for sure. Where would they find a crafting table, or diamonds? He took a deep breath.

"Uh, oh." Charli pointed. At the furthest point they could see, a bright yellow object sank toward the horizon. The sky surrounding it was turning orange, the sky above purple.

"The sun's setting," JJ said.

"Setting?" Annie spoke quietly, too afraid to say the words without whispering. "Nighttime equals mobs."

"Yep." Jamie bounced from foot to foot, a wide grin on his face. "Imagine seeing a creeper or a zombie. No one's going to believe us."

"Believe us? Who cares if anyone believes us?" Charli took a deep breath. She looked as worried as Annie. "The mobs can kill us, Jamie. Stop smiling and be serious. We're in real trouble."

CHAPTER THREE

An Unwelcome Night

Jamie's smile disappeared. At last he seemed to understand they were in danger. "Can we respawn?" he asked.

"We can't risk trying to find out," JJ said. "For now we need to find somewhere safe to sleep. The mobs will be gone again in the morning."

"What about the house?" Charli asked. "We could sleep there."

"The house is miles away," Jamie said. "How do we get there?"

"Sprint," Charli said. "Follow me." Without waiting for any of them to argue she walked down the hill.

JJ, Annie, and Jamie stayed close to her. The soft grass crunched beneath their feet.

"How do we sprint?" Annie asked.

"I'm not sure," JJ said. "Keep walking. We'll work things out as we go." He followed Charli in the direction of the house. Cows, chickens, pigs, and sheep roamed the landscape as they walked.

They passed a river, climbed a small rocky mountain, and continued toward a forest. They were only halfway to the house when the sun sank completely below the horizon.

A gust of wind almost knocked JJ off his feet as Jamie streaked past, his left arm outstretched as he sprinted.

JJ called out to him. "Jamie, stop." A dust cloud formed on the path ahead. When it settled, JJ could see his brother waiting for them to catch up.

Jamie grinned. "Punch your left arm out twice. Second time, hold it out and you'll sprint."

JJ followed Jamie's instructions and found himself sprinting. He stopped and turned to check on the others. They were a long way behind. A cloud of dust in the distance blocked his view.

He waited until one, two, three bodies zipped past him. He thrust his arm out twice and chased after them.

They didn't stop until they reached the house. Only torches lit the perimeter. The mountain behind stood in darkness.

"The torches should keep the mobs away," JJ said. "Now quick, everyone get inside." He moved to the front door and punched at the button. The iron door didn't open.

Jamie moved in front of him and hit the button. This time the door opened. He pushed the girls and JJ inside before following them into the house. The door slammed behind them.

JJ stared at the door. "How did you get the door open when I couldn't?"

"Wrong hand." Jamie held up his right hand, "Think of your hands as the controller buttons. They seem to do the same thing. And look," he pointed to the floor, "a pressure pad. Stand on it and the door closes."

JJ nodded. Jamie surprised him. He wasn't used to his little brother knowing more than he did.

Annie's teeth chattered pulling him from his thoughts.

"You're okay Annie," he said. "We're safe now."

"What if any creatures get in?"

"They won't," JJ said. "We did a good job of building the house, it's secure. Now let's find the beds. We need to go to sleep."

"Can we look at my library or the movie theater first?" Charli asked.

"No, let's wait until morning." JJ

walked to the bedroom. "Morning will come quicker if we sleep."

For once, Charli didn't argue. She followed with Jamie and Annie close behind her.

JJ wondered how long nighttime would take. Had his dad realized they were missing yet? Their priority was to get to bed and wait until morning. He'd have to deal with his parents, and maybe even the police, once they got home. He swallowed. Once they got home. Didn't he mean if they got home?

∽

JJ lay down on the bed. He worried mobs might be present, preventing him from sleeping. But, a short time after lying down, the sky lightened and the sun began to rise. Morning approached.

"I wish night was that short back home," Jamie said. "Imagine all the extra game time we'd get." He stood. "Let's go outside."

"What about mobs?" Annie asked. "Shouldn't we wait? They might kill us."

"The sun burns up most of them," JJ said. "We can always run back in if anything's out there."

Jamie led them through the house and back downstairs.

Charli stopped at the library door. "One quick look. Okay?" She pushed the door open and stepped inside. Bookshelves lined the walls from the floor to the ceiling. Every shelf was filled with books.

"The books are real," Annie said. "Look." She picked one up and flicked through it.

After a few minutes, Jamie spoke. "Come on. I thought you wanted to get home. We need to start work on the portal."

Annie put the book back in its place. "You're right, let's go."

JJ and Charli followed them out through the front door. Brilliant sunshine lit the Minecraft world.

They walked out to the deck. JJ stopped and looked out at the land and lake surrounding the house. "Shame we didn't build the moat and my trap to drown mobs. I think—" He stopped, a lump caught in his throat. A creeper was right behind Jamie and Annie. As they walked along the side of the house, it moved from the long grass toward them. "Jamie, Annie, run!"

Annie rushed to JJ. Jamie ignored the warning and turned to look at the creeper.

"Jamie!" JJ's heart pounded so hard he thought his chest might explode. Jamie was in serious trouble.

The creeper moved next to the house. Its body flashed white and it emitted a hissing sound. Jamie punched the air twice and tried to sprint. Something was wrong. He was walking at normal speed.

An explosion erupted when Jamie was halfway to them, knocking him from his feet.

Annie grabbed on to JJ to keep from falling. The ground shook. Smoke poured from the side of the house. After a few moments it cleared. JJ pulled Jamie to his feet and turned to look at the damage. The window facing onto the garden had been blown apart, leaving a massive hole.

❧

"Look at the side of the house," Charli said. "Blown to bits. Lucky it wasn't you, Jamie."

Jamie stared in shock at the hole.

"Are there more?" Annie asked.

JJ surveyed the area. "I hope not. But look…"

Bones littered the ground.

"Skeletons?" Charli asked.

JJ nodded. "Yes, definitely skeletons. The sun's burned these guys up. Come on, we've got to get started on the portal. With a huge hole in the house we aren't going to keep the mobs out tonight."

"I don't think I can," Charli said. "I'm so hungry."

"Me too," Annie said.

"Me three." Jamie punched his arm, his inventory pad appearing. "My hunger bar is nearly empty. Three bars left. That's why I couldn't sprint."

"If we don't find some food, creepers will be the least of our issues," JJ said.

"We ran past some cows yesterday," Jamie said. "They're not far, even walking to them will be quick."

"What are you going to do, kill

them?" Annie looked horrified.

"Of course, how else are we going to eat? Let's go." Jamie walked in the direction of the cows. After a few steps he turned and walked back. "I'm going to collect these first," he said, "turning them into bone meal and planting crops can be our backup plan. Bone meal is an amazing fertilizer." He picked up the bones from the ground around him before walking off again.

"Come on," JJ said to the girls. "Stick together in case any mobs are still around."

JJ, Annie, and Charli followed Jamie's lead. Moments later they all stopped. Cows surrounded them.

"Wow, they look like real cows,"

Charli said. "And they stink. What's that awful smell?"

"Yuk," Jamie said. "Cow poo. Good thing you can't smell through a screen, no one would play Minecraft. Now, come here pretty girl." He moved toward a large brown and white cow, his right arm raised, ready to punch her.

"Stop," Annie said. "You can't hit her, she's a real cow."

Jamie looked at her. "Sorry Annie," he turned back to the cow, "we have no choice, we need to eat."

"I can't be part of this. I'm going back to the house." Annie turned and walked away.

Jamie raised his arm again and punched the cow in the head.

The cow bellowed the moment Jamie's fist connected. She staggered to one side, losing control of her back legs. She nearly fell over but managed to straighten herself.

Jamie froze. The cow continued to moo, she was hurt. His eyes filled with tears. She tried to walk away but kept swaying as if she would fall. Her sad eyes looked at Jamie. He walked closer to her and she bellowed louder. She blinked, frightened. He put his hand out and stroked her nose. "I'm so sorry, I didn't think you would get hurt." The cow nuzzled into his hand.

"I think she's forgiven you," JJ said, as the cow rubbed against Jamie. "Let's not hit animals again."

Jamie nodded. "If one punch hurt her so much, imagine if we get hurt. We might not respawn."

"Let's hope we don't find out," Charli said. "It could be a disaster."

"Come on, we should get Annie." JJ turned toward the house. "We need to stay together and find some food."

Jamie patted the cow one last time and the three made their way back to the house. Their stomachs groaned, their hunger bars had weakened further.

"How many bones did you get?" JJ asked as they walked. "I think we need to move to your backup plan."

"Heaps, so we've got plenty of bone meal. We can use the grass seeds we got yesterday to grow the wheat, harvest it, and make bread."

"We'll need to work out how to make a hoe as well," JJ said.

"And a crafting table," Jamie said. "We can use the wood I collected yesterday. Let's get Annie and go and make one."

Charli called for Annie as they reached the front door of the house. "Where are you?"

Annie didn't answer.

"Do you think she's okay?" Jamie asked. "I wish I'd never suggested going after the cows. The cow got hurt, Annie's mad at me, and now we're all starving. Let's find her so I can say sorry."

They walked inside the house. In the movie theater, grinning from car to car, they found Annie eating a giant cake.

CHAPTER FOUR

Teamwork

JJ couldn't believe his eyes. They were all starving and here was Annie, happily eating a cake.

She stopped chewing, her smile replaced by a frown. "I found some food. Sorry, but I'm not killing animals with my hands. I'll stick to cake instead."

"But how did you find cake?" JJ said.

"I made bread and cake, remember, while you guys built the house."

"At my house, on the Xbox?"

Annie nodded. "I put it in the movie theater."

"That's right, she did too," Charli said. "Remember when we went on the tour of the house? You said to leave the food here for the people watching movies."

"How much do you have?" JJ asked.

Annie punched her sleeve and her inventory pad came out. "I picked everything up so there's four cakes, eight apples, and twelve loaves of bread. I should be okay for days."

"What about us?" Jamie's nostrils flared, his face red.

"Didn't you eat the cow?"

"The first punch hurt her too much, we couldn't kill her," JJ said. "Come on, split the food up, we're all so weak."

"I'll give you two apples and three loaves each, okay? The cakes are mine, I spent ages making them."

"And we spent ages making this house, which kept us safe last night," Jamie said. "Imagine if you couldn't come in because you hadn't helped. Do you think you'd still be alive?"

"This is no time to argue," JJ said. "Annie, divide the food, please. Everyone needs to be at full strength and we all need to work as a team."

Annie reluctantly threw the food from her inventory. The other three scooped it up and started eating.

"Mm, yum. This is delicious, so delicious," Charli said.

"Don't waste any," JJ said. "Only eat until your hunger bar is restored. We'll keep the rest for later, in case we run low again. Annie, Jamie has an idea to plant wheat and make bread, but first we need to make a crafting table."

"Come on." Jamie walked back out the door. "Let's get to work."

⚬

JJ and the girls followed Jamie out of the house. Jamie's attitude amazed JJ. He might be the youngest but he was thinking through problems, he had become a leader. JJ was proud of him.

"Come on, we need a crafting table," Jamie said.

"Why are we doing this?" Annie

asked. "Our hunger bars are full."

"Yeah, but what if they run out again?" Charli said. "We've only got a small amount of food left."

"We don't need the crafting table just for food," Jamie said. "If we're going to make a portal we'll need a diamond pickaxe. Do you realize how hard diamonds are to find?"

"Why did we build the stupid house in survival mode?" Charli asked. "If we'd played in creative this would be so much easier."

"Survival is a challenge, that's why," JJ said. "We can't do anything about which mode we're in now so let's get moving."

Jamie opened his inventory pad and switched it on. "I've still got heaps of wood left. Let's see what happens if I move some into the crafting squares." He dragged the wood blocks into the four crafting squares with his finger. Wood planks immediately floated in front of him.

"Amazing," Charli said. "Can you do it again?"

Jamie added blocks of wood to the crafting squares and more wood planks appeared.

"We need to put the planks back in the squares to make the table," JJ said. "You won't need all of them."

Jamie walked into the planks, watching as they disappeared. He placed one into each of the four crafting squares. A crafting table appeared in the box next to them and he moved it down into his inventory. The dust on the ground beside them swirled, slowly at first, then faster and faster.

"What's happening?" Annie shouted over the noise of the wind.

They covered their eyes as the dust churned around them. It was impossible to see. Annie grabbed JJ's arm, holding on while the wind blew them back and forth. Suddenly everything stopped.

They opened their eyes. A table with nine holes in the top stood before them.

"A crafting table," Jamie said. "We actually did it."

"Look at the holes," Charli said. "Do you think we put materials in them to craft things?"

"One way to find out," JJ said. "We need a hoe. Jamie's still got plenty of wood. Let's make some sticks and then try to make one. Throw out the extra planks from your inventory. You'll need to place them in the right squares of the crafting table. Put one on the second line, the other needs to go on the third line, directly underneath it."

Jamie followed JJ's instructions. Nothing happened. He turned to face JJ and the girls. "That didn't work. Any other—" The wind picked up with a deafening roar, cutting Jamie off. Dust flew everywhere. The crafting table rose off the ground. It spun faster as the wind lashed around it. The dust became too much for them and they turned away and closed their eyes. Moments later, the dust settled and they turned back around, eyes open. The crafting table stood in front of them, four sticks on top.

"Yes!" Jamie jumped up and down. "Come on, let's put the sticks in with more wood planks and make the hoe."

Once again the table took the items. The wind and dirt swirled and the table spun above them, so fast they could no longer watch.

CHAPTER FIVE

New Discoveries

JJ stared at the crafting table. They'd made a hoe. As long as they found the raw materials, and remembered where to put them on the table, they would be able to make whatever they needed.

Annie walked over to the table and picked up the hoe. "Let's find a good spot to prepare the ground and plant the seeds," she said.

JJ looked at her and smiled. She looked relaxed, almost happy. "We're in your area of expertise now," he said.

Annie laughed. "I may not be good at building mansions, fighting zombies, or finding the right armor, but food… with food I'm a Minecraft master." She pointed to the house. "Let's go around the back. We can use the large grassy area and the lake will supply the water we'll need." She walked around the side of the house, Jamie and Charli by her side.

JJ punched the crafting table before following them. It smashed into small pieces and disappeared as they touched his skin. He hurried and caught up to the others.

Jamie's head turned in the direction of the lookout tower as he followed Annie. He stopped. "You guys plant the seeds while I go up and take a look. I want to see what's in the distance."

"Okay, but be quick," JJ said. "Give me the bones before you go. We'll get the wheat growing and make bread before we start on the portal."

Jamie converted the bones to bone meal. He threw the materials on the ground for JJ and ran to the tower.

Annie used the hoe to prepare the area. Planting the seeds and coating them with bone meal took only moments.

"Look," Charli said, "the seeds are sprouting."

"They're more than sprouting." JJ said. The seedlings grew bigger and bigger before turning into full grown wheat. "This is amazing." He imagined his dad's reaction if his vegetable patch grew as quickly.

"Time to harvest," JJ said.

Annie and Charli moved into the field and punched the wheat. JJ walked with them, collecting the floating pieces for his inventory.

"Hey guys, guess what?" Jamie ran over to them. "I saw a village. Over those hills." He pointed into the distance. "A real village."

"Village? Really?" JJ didn't remember seeing a village when they'd played the Xbox map.

"Yes, we should go and visit." Jamie turned to run.

"No, wait." JJ stepped in front of his brother. "We can't go now."

"Why? I want to explore and meet a villager."

"We need to build a portal. We don't have time."

Jamie hesitated. "What if a portal already exists? Would we have time to go to the village?"

"If you've found a portal, tell us now." The sun would start sinking again soon. "With the hole in the house we'll be in danger when nighttime arrives. We need to build a portal or repair the house before we do anything else."

"But what about the village?"

JJ stared at his brother. "We're not going to the village. Tell us about the portal. It might be the difference between us getting home or not."

"If I tell you and we get back home, I need you to promise we'll come in again."

JJ nodded. "Okay."

"What?" Annie shrieked. "No way am I coming back and Charli's not either."

"Hold on, I might want to come back," Charli said.

"Stop. Everybody stop." JJ held up his hands. "Let's get home first before we worry about coming back. Jamie, where's the portal?"

Jamie kicked at the rock next to him. "Fine. Halfway between here and the village there's something like a portal sitting between a waterfall and a lake."

"For real?" JJ asked.

Jamie nodded.

The other three exchanged a look.

"Hey, stop!" Jamie said. "What are you doing?"

JJ, Annie, and Charli didn't answer, they grabbed Jamie's arms and started sprinting.

᪻

The purple light of the portal flickered in the afternoon sunlight. The magnificent waterfall started high up on the mountain, its water cascading down to the lake beside them.

"The village is close to here," Jamie said. "Why don't we quickly visit before we go through the portal?"

JJ shook his head. "No time. We need to get out of here before nighttime and mobs arrive."

"We can get to the village and back before nighttime," Jamie said.

"Okay," JJ agreed. "If you can show me how you plan to get to the portal, I'll consider going."

Jamie looked confused. "What do you mean?" He pointed. "The portal's right here."

"Yes. Right here, surrounded by a lava moat."

"So? We jump across."

"Are you crazy? What if one of us falls in?"

"We won't. We'll be fine."

"I'm not jumping across lava," Annie said, "it's hot enough just standing here. We'll be fried."

"I'll jump across and prove you won't

get fried." Jamie moved closer to the lava moat.

"No," JJ said. "It's too hot." He doubted anyone would be able to get close enough to jump.

"If I run fast enough before I jump the heat won't matter."

"No," JJ said. "It's too big a risk."

Frustration crossed Jamie's face. "So what then? Are we back to building another portal? That's crazy when we've got one sitting right in front of us."

"Of course we're going to use it," JJ said. "We should be able to throw dirt on top of the lava and walk across."

"Do we just punch the ground to get dirt?" Charli asked.

"One way to find out," Jamie said.

He started punching at the ground in front of him. It took a few punches until a dirt block floated above the ground.

"Easy." JJ grinned. "Come on, collect four blocks each, that should be enough." Working as a team it only took a couple of minutes before they had collected all the dirt blocks they needed.

"I'll put a block in first and check that it works," JJ said. He moved closer to the lava and shielded his face. "It's so hot, this is as close as I can get." JJ threw a dirt block toward the lava. It landed on the ground before reaching the moat. He threw another. It didn't reach.

"I'll try," Jamie said. He threw one of his blocks and it too fell short of the lava. He tried again and so did Charli. None of the blocks reached.

"What do we do now?" Annie asked. "If the lava's too hot we won't be able to use the portal."

JJ looked around for an answer. The portal was right in front of them, it would be crazy not to use it, but how were they going to get across the lava?

"Can we fly over it?" Charli asked.

"Not in survival mode," JJ said. "If we were in creative we could. I'm thinking of another option. We'll need iron." His eyes searched their surroundings. He sprinted away from the group toward the mountain. He got halfway around it before he found what he was looking for and returned. "Okay, here's my idea. We make a bucket and throw water on the lava. Water won't be as heavy to throw as dirt. If we wet ourselves down we won't feel the heat as much, we should be able to get closer to the moat. The lava will turn to cobblestone or obsidian and we can walk across to the portal."

"Great plan," Annie said. "So how do we make a bucket?"

"By mining for iron ore and using a furnace to smelt it into ingots. We'll need three ingots." JJ pointed at the mountain. "Around the side I found a cave, it will be our quickest way to find the ore." He looked at Jamie. "I'll need your help."

Jamie continued to stare at the bubbling orange moat.

"Even if you made it, one of us might slip and fall. Do you want to be responsible for that?" JJ could see his brother still wanted to jump.

Jamie shook his head. "I'll help make the bucket. We're going to need a stone pickaxe too."

JJ smiled. The many hours the two brothers spent playing Minecraft were paying off. "Okay, let's get started. We're going to need torches to light up the cave. How much wood is left?"

Jamie checked his inventory. "I have forty-eight blocks of wood and nineteen sticks."

"Perfect. Let's make the pickaxe first. We can turn the wood to charcoal and make some torches, finding coal will take too long."

JJ accessed his inventory pad and

pressed on the crafting table. Immediately the wind began to blow. They shut their eyes against the elements. Calm soon arrived and so did the crafting table.

"First step," JJ took charge, "is to make a wooden pickaxe and turn it into a stone one. Jamie, put the items into the crafting table."

Jamie threw three wood blocks and two sticks from his inventory to the ground in front of him. He picked up each item and put it into the table. Three wood blocks in the top squares, one stick in the middle square, and one in the bottom square. The wind increased and swirled around them.

Charli shouted over the noise. "Here we go."

The wind sucked up the table, spinning faster and faster. Dust whipped around them, flying into their faces, forcing their eyes shut. The calm returned and they opened their eyes. The wooden pickaxe they'd created floated above the table.

"Awesome." Jamie picked up the pickaxe. "I'll go and mine some cobblestone to make a stone pickaxe."

"Get enough for the furnace too," JJ said. "You'll need three blocks for the pickaxe and eight for the furnace. Get extra, we should probably make a spare pickaxe."

"How do you remember the exact numbers of everything?" Annie asked.

JJ laughed. "These are pretty basic

tools, so you'd remember most of them yourself."

Annie shook her head. "I doubt it."

"I bet you've memorized the ingredients for a cake," JJ said.

A pink flush crept across Annie's cheeks. "I guess we remember what we're interested in."

"Jamie's on his way back." Charli pointed at Jamie who hurried toward them.

"I got cobblestone," he said.

It didn't take long to create a stone pickaxe and a furnace. Jamie retrieved the pickaxe and added more sticks and cobblestone to the table.

"What are you doing?" Annie asked.

"One pickaxe might not be enough."

He made another three pickaxes and threw two to JJ.

JJ walked into them, still fascinated by the way they disappeared. "Next job, let's make some charcoal for the torches. Then we'll be ready to get into the cave and find some iron ore."

"This is a lot of effort for a bucket," Jamie said. "Jumping across the lava would be a million times quicker."

JJ ignored him. No one would jump, no matter how many times it was suggested. "We'll need about five charcoal pieces. That will give us twenty torches."

Jamie placed five wood blocks in the top of the furnace and a pile of planks in the bottom hole, to act as fuel. He jumped back as the planks ignited. They crackled and burned as the furnace heated up. Smoke billowed around them.

"Wow, that's hot," Charli said.

Annie coughed. "Are you sure this is what's supposed to happen?" She moved back and the others moved with her.

When the smoke cleared a small fire remained. Five pieces of charcoal floated above it.

They returned to the crafting table and Jamie added the materials. Following a whirlwind of dust and massive winds, twenty torches appeared.

"Great job," JJ said. "Now we're ready to explore the cave."

Jamie shook his head. "Not quite." He added a stick and two cobblestones to the crafting table. When the wind stopped and the dust had settled, a stone sword floated above the table. Jamie repeated the process, quickly crafting a second. He passed one to JJ and added one to his inventory. "Okay, now we're ready."

CHAPTER SIX

Surviving Underground

All four gathered at the entrance of the dark cave.

Annie stopped. "I don't want to go."

"That's fine," JJ said. "Wait by the entrance for us. If the sun starts setting yell down or come and tell us."

"Charli, can you wait with me?" Annie asked. "I don't want to wait here alone."

"Okay," Charli said.

"Really?" JJ was sure she'd put up a

fight to go into the cave. "I thought you'd want to go?"

"It's safer if we all go or if we stay in groups of two," Charli said. "Yes, I'd like to go and explore but if anyone stays it makes sense it's me. Identifying rock types isn't my strength. It's the one thing I'll admit you and Jamie are better at."

JJ smiled. That Charli would admit he was good at something was a first.

"We'll make some bread while you're gone. We've run out of food and will need to eat soon."

"Great idea." JJ took the wheat from his inventory and Charli collected it.

"The crafting table is still by the waterfall," JJ said.

Annie and Charli walked over to the

crafting table while JJ and Jamie entered the cave.

"Stay close," JJ said, "and place torches when it gets too dark."

They cave's natural path led them down into the earth. The darkness increased with each step they took and, when Jamie placed the first torch, relief flooded through JJ. The passage ahead of him lit up. "I can see coal in the rocks here, heaps of it." He hacked at it with his pickaxe, watching as the stone broke and the coal floated in front of him. "I'll get a bit for making more torches." JJ collected ten pieces before he stopped. "Let's keep going, we need iron ore."

Jamie placed another torch as they moved deeper underground.

JJ stopped abruptly and turned, he raised a finger to his lips. They stood and listened. A strange sound came from up ahead.

"What's that?" Jamie said.

JJ kept his voice low. "I'm not sure, but it's getting louder."

Jamie nodded. "It sounds like paper being ripped in half or a weird kind of snake hissing."

JJ realized what it was. "Let's get out of here," he said, ready to hurry out of the cave. "It's a cave spider, it'll kill us."

Jamie didn't move. "Look." He pointed to the roof. The gray blocks contained brown spots. "Iron ore."

The spider's dreaded hissing was getting closer. Its red, glowing eyes lit up the end of the tunnel.

JJ moved his legs, trying to stop their trembling. Was Jamie's heartbeat racing like his? "The spider's too close. We need to think of another plan."

"No way." Jamie pushed in front of JJ, his stone sword outstretched. "Take this you rotten spider." He lunged at the spider. He slashed the sword back and forth, hitting it again and again. Each time the blade connected the spider hissed and screeched. Finally, the noise stopped. The spider disappeared, leaving string and a spider eye floating in its place.

"I killed it! Did you see me? I actually killed it." Jamie jumped up and down, excitement overtaking him.

JJ stood, rooted to the spot. His little brother, the same boy who'd almost cried when he'd punched the cow, was now ecstatic he'd killed something. "It's dead," was all he managed to say.

Jamie stopped jumping. "I killed it before it killed us. Now come on, let's get the iron and get out of here. We don't know what else is around." He switched his sword for a pickaxe and hacked at the blocks.

JJ watched him for a moment before picking up his own pickaxe. It hadn't been a harmless cow. It was a mob. A mob that, given the chance, would have killed them.

When JJ and Jamie emerged from the cave they found Charli and Annie waiting by the waterfall.

"How did you go?" Charli asked. "Did you find iron?"

"Yes," JJ said. "We've got heaps. Enough to make ten buckets. A few exciting things happened along the way, didn't they Jamie?"

Jamie nodded. "We'll tell you everything once we get home. Our priority now is to make a bucket. I need to eat first though. My hunger bar is getting low again. Did you make any bread?"

"Thirty pieces," Annie said. "Here you go." She threw some pieces to the boys. They collected them and ate until their hunger bars were restored.

"Time to make the bucket," JJ said. "We need to turn the iron ore into ingots. We found some coal in the cave too, so we can use it for heating the furnace."

"No need," Charli said. "We collected wood and turned it into planks while you were gone. We've got plenty of fuel."

JJ smiled at the girls. Everyone was working as a team. "Okay, let's get to work and smelt the ingots."

Charli put the wood planks in the bottom of the furnace and JJ put the iron ore blocks in the top. The furnace heated up once again, black smoke billowing everywhere. In no time the smoke cleared and an iron ingot appeared. They repeated the process until they had made three ingots.

JJ coughed as he collected them. "Lucky we only need one bucket. One should be enough to do the job and that saves us having to breathe in more smoke." He moved to the crafting table and added the ingots. He closed his eyes as the dust and wind swirled around.

"You did it," Annie said. "You made a bucket!"

JJ opened his eyes to find a bucket floating calmly in front of him. He picked it up and smiled at the others. "You mean we did it. Great effort guys." He walked to the waterfall and filled the bucket. "Now let's see if we can make this work."

The heat from the lava made it impossible to get too close to the moat. JJ put the bucket down and walked back to the waterfall. He stood under the spray. Now drenched, he collected the bucket and inched closer to the lava. When he was too hot to move further JJ threw the water. Steam rose as it landed on the lava.

He grinned. "It worked, and look, the lava's turned to obsidian."

"Awesome." Jamie stepped toward the moat. "The obsidian is much cooler than the lava. We'll only need a few blocks, just enough to walk across."

JJ nodded. He collected more water from the waterfall and threw it onto the lava. He repeated this another seven times. A safe path of obsidian now led to the portal.

∽

"I'm still going to jump," Jamie said.

JJ couldn't believe his ears. All the hard work to make a safe path and Jamie still wanted to risk his life.

Jamie laughed. "Not the lava, the obsidian. I'm going to prove jumping over is possible."

The other three watched as Jamie walked back to get a running start. He raced toward the moat and leaped. He landed on one of the obsidian blocks.

"Dead," JJ said. "You would be dead."

Jamie shook his head. His shoulders slumped as he crossed to the safety of the portal. "Lucky you didn't listen to me," he said, as the others joined him.

"You're lucky," Annie said. "None of us would have tried. You would have gone first and landed in lava. A pretty good warning for the rest of us."

"Let's not think about what might have happened," JJ said. "Let's go home."

Charli hesitated. "Why would a portal be sitting here?"

"Maybe the Wilson brothers used it to get home," JJ said.

"But how did they use the portal with lava all around it?"

"Maybe they could fly," Jamie said. "They might have been in creative mode."

"We don't even know if they entered this map," Annie said. "Who cares how it got here? The main thing is we found it. Let's see if we can get home."

"What if we end up in the Nether or another map?" Charli asked.

"We won't know until we go," JJ said. "Now you three go. I'll follow you."

"I'm staying," Jamie said. "I want to explore. I know where the portal is so I can get out whenever I need to."

JJ shook his head. "No. We don't even know where this is going to take us. Wherever it goes, we all go together. The sun's beginning to sink again."

"Yeah, come on." Annie grabbed hold of Jamie's arm, Charli took the other and, between them, the girls dragged him into the bright purple light.

They disappeared instantly.

CHAPTER SEVEN

The Doorway Home

JJ took one last look at the world around him and stepped into the purple light. Sucked in and propelled forward through bright flashing lights the colors vanished and his focus cleared. He stood in the forest behind his house.

Jamie, Annie, and Charli waited for him. Their Minecraft skins were gone and they all looked like their regular selves.

JJ looked down, he was back to normal too. "Did that really happen?"

"Yep. Sure did," Charli said. "What do we do now?"

"Go home," Annie said. "Everyone's going to be worried. We've been gone for ages. Days even."

"What day is it?" Jamie asked.

None of them knew.

A voice filtered through the forest.

"Your dad's calling." Charli turned to JJ. "He's probably got a search party out looking for us."

"Quick, let's go before he finds the portal," JJ said.

They followed JJ's lead and ran through the clearing toward the creek and forest.

The voice became louder and clearer as they got closer to home. "JJ, Jamie,

Charli, Annie, food's ready."

"Coming," JJ yelled. He lowered his voice to speak to the others. "So much for a search party. He was getting food organized when we left. Maybe time hasn't passed at all."

"Or it's gone slowly," Annie said.

"So no one will be looking for us," Charli said. "Good. They're not going to believe us if we tell them where we've been."

"No one can tell them anything," Jamie said. "We'd never be allowed back."

"Back?" Annie gasped. "No way am I going back. No way at all."

"But what about the village? Don't you want to go and meet the villagers?" Jamie asked. "I do."

Annie shook her head. "Nope, never. Now let's go and eat. We might be back in the real world but my hunger bar is still very low."

"The cake we ate in the map was better than this," Annie said.

"Try some cheese and crackers." JJ passed her the second plate of food. "Now, we should agree on some rules about what happened."

"Why?" Annie asked.

"Because we don't want anyone finding out," Jamie said. "This needs to be our secret."

"Yes, and no one is to go back in unless we're all together," JJ said. "Does everyone understand?"

Jamie and the girls nodded.

"Except I don't want to go back," Annie said.

"Okay, you don't have to," JJ said. "How about we tell you when we go. That way if we don't come back, you can tell my parents."

"And say what? They won't believe me. They'll think I'm crazy, that you've all been kidnapped."

JJ frowned, she was right. They might think she was crazy, though the portal was pretty convincing. "Don't worry for now. Let's agree to stay away from the forest until we've worked out the details. Okay?"

The other three nodded. Their adventure would remain a secret.

"Do you think they'll keep the secret?" Jamie asked. The two boys lay in bed. They'd moved Jamie's mattress into JJ's room for a sleepover.

"Probably," JJ said. "No one would believe them. If they did tell the truth we could deny everything. They'd look crazy. The only real problem would be if someone else is shown, or finds the portal. Luckily the forest is so thick."

"I want to go back in," Jamie said. "You'll come too, won't you?"

JJ shook his head. "I don't think we should rush back in. We had a pretty close call in the end. It's dangerous and we don't know if we can respawn."

"We might. Let's get one of the girls to die and test it."

JJ laughed. "I can't see either of them volunteering for the job. What if they didn't respawn and died in this world too? That would be awful."

"So you and I go back and visit the village without them," Jamie said.

"Let's talk about it later. We agreed no one would go in alone and we would decide as a group what to do about the portal. Charli's got a basketball tournament tomorrow, so let's have a club meeting on Sunday. We can chat about everything then." JJ didn't wait for Jamie to respond and turned off the light. "Now, I'm exhausted, goodnight."

Jamie snuggled down under his

blanket. Sunday? He couldn't wait until Sunday. He was dying to go to the village. Meeting a villager would be awesome. He lay with his eyes open, grateful he didn't have to worry about creepers or any other mobs tonight. He didn't care what agreement the others had made. One adventure might be enough for them but it wasn't enough for him.

He was going back in.

Books currently available in The Crafters' Club Series

Two Worlds
The Villagers
Lost
The Professor
Spirit
Friendship

Are you dying to know whether Jamie goes back through the portal alone? Will he visit the village and meet a villager? Book Two in The Crafters' Club Series, The Villagers, is now available for purchase in both print and eBook versions. Read the first chapter for free when you join The Crafters' Club!

Visit TheCraftersClub.com to purchase your copy of The Villagers. Alternatively, chat with your favorite book retailer to order your copy.

Join The Crafters' Club – It's Free!

You too can join JJ, Jamie, Annie, and Charli as a member of The Crafters' Club. Prizes, special offers and advance notice of new book releases are just some of the benefits of belonging to the club. Sign up for free today at:

www.TheCraftersClub.com

Acknowledgments

Thank you to Ray and our two boys for their knowledge and instruction on all things Minecraft. Without your interest and enthusiasm The Crafters' Club would not exist. An extra thank you to Ray for your support, encouragement, and input to the Crafters' Club series. Your website concept and design is outstanding.

A very special thank you to Minecraft fans, and avid readers, Finn and Lyell, for their feedback on early drafts of the story. To Sally Odgers, thank you for your input, and to Judy and Tash, a huge thank you for your well-utilized proofreading services.

Sincere thanks to Kathy Betts of Element Editing Services for your thorough editing and improvement of this story.

Finally, thanks to Lana Pecherczyk for her wonderful illustrations and cover design.